Tea and Biscuits

A. L. KENNEDY

A Phoenix Paperback

Tea and Biscuits first appeared in *Original Prints III* (Polygon)
Night Geometry and the Garscadden Trains first appeared in
Beloit Fiction Journal, Vol 5, No 1
Bix first appeared in *Night Geometry and the Garscadden Trains* in 1990
published by Polygon *The Seaside Photographer* first appeared in
Edinburgh Review, 83
Genteel Potatoes first appeared in *Bête Noire*, 7

This edition published in 1996 by Phoenix
a division of Orion Books Ltd
Orion House, 5 Upper St Martin's Lane, London WC2H 9EA

ISBN 1 85799 757 3

Typeset by Deltatype Ltd, Ellesmere Port, Cheshire
Printed in Great Britain by Clays Ltd, St Ives plc

CONTENTS

Tea and Biscuits

I went to visit him, late because I had to drive slowly, but I ran all the stairs to make up. He opened the door and I'll tell you what we said.

'You smell the kettle boiling?'

'That's right.'

'Well, do come in.'

'Thank you. Thanks a lot.'

The flat was very like him; in his colours, with his books, his jacket on a chair in the living room. I recognised that. It was warm in there. He must have been home for a while, sitting near the fire with the paper perhaps, and the sleeves of his shirt rolled up.

'Come and talk to me, then.'

'Hn?'

'I'll show my kitchen to you. Come on.'

I was wearing stockings. I like them, because they feel good, but I thought that he would like them, too. I didn't imagine he would see them, or that he would know I had them on, but I thought that he would like them if he did.

Nothing in his kitchen had names on, not even the coffee

and tea. Some of it was in jars that you could see through, but for the rest, you would have to remember where everything was. There were ones that he always forgot: rice and porridge, oats and macaroni. I didn't know that then.

When Michael made us coffee he almost gave me sugar as if he expected I'd take it because he did. In the same way, later, I would see him pick up a book and feel it was strange when he didn't put glasses on.

I noticed, back in the living room, when he bent to turn down the fire, that the grey by his temples had faded to white. The cherry light from the gas shone round his head and the hairs that would be pale in daylight showed more red. He was no nearer balding than I remembered – hardly even thin – but his colours were changed, now. I saw that.

My grandfather was in hospital once, a long time ago. Very ill, and though nobody said so, I think he'd had a heart attack. I was taken to visit, just Gran and me, and I saw a stranger in his bed. He wore new, stripey cotton pyjamas. They were something from home and didn't suit the sheets. His head was low in the pillows and I could see his throat, soft and loose where he swallowed. Out of his shirt and pullover he wasn't like my grandfather at all. He was like anyone. Just a man lying down.

I kissed him goodbye and it felt like kissing a man. It felt funny, like when you think of Jesus or a minister being a man. It was like that. I felt guilty. I was seeing him in the way a stranger would. I was seeing his illness. I sat and looked at the bedspread and wasn't nice to him and left, knowing I'd let us both down.

I thought that in the morning our waking would be something like that. Between Michael and me. I thought that I would turn and look at him and see I had wasted it all, that an ageing man I'd once admired would be sleeping, maybe snoring at my side. He would smell of old sweat. I would see that the muscles in his arms were beginning to sink and be frightened by an old face, older in sleep. Slack.

I was wrong; selfish too. Probably selfish.

The warmth of his stomach was fitted against my back and his legs behind my legs were nice, just right. Perhaps his movement had disturbed me, I don't know, but however it happened, it was easy and that was me awake. I answered him with a voice I hadn't heard before, my thoughts running on and feeling new and, as I turned for his arm, I didn't doubt that I could look at him safely and find good. Something good would be there. I wanted him to see as much in me.

He kissed me, I think on the nose, and said 'Good morning.'

'Come here. I want to tell you. I love you.'

'That's nice.'

There are different and better ways to say it. Anything I've ever thought of has seemed to be second hand; something you might have stolen from Tammy Wynette. I should have said that when he ran, and he often did, he ran like nobody else and I loved him for that. He had a rhythm and blues kind of run. Pale socks. I should have said I loved him for every time, but most of all for my first, because he made it a gift and a thing to remember and he was sweet.

That morning was strange. We sat up in bed, recovering slowly, and looked at it and declared it all to be extremely odd. Herring gulls heading to sea again, flying soft and heavy up the street and a light behind the paper shop window, but no sound. The street lamps whispered out below us and the last of the night wore away while Michael brought me tea in bed as if I was somehow fragile after the night.

'How are you feeling?'

'Very nice.'

'You don't hurt?'

'No. I ache a bit.'

'Where?'

'You want me to show you?'

'I'm going to have trouble with you.'

I told him that I'd missed the Sixties, and I felt I had a lot to make up. All that permissiveness.

'You missed nothing. Move over, I'm getting cold.'

Perhaps what surprised us both was our luck. When I was still his student we could have tried it, had the affair, plenty of other people always did. There were even two or three times when it could have started, like when my father died and Michael was so nice. He told me that it wouldn't get better, but I could manage it a day at a time. He could have been more sympathetic and tried to get more in return. We could have let it happen then and lasted a couple of terms, maybe more. Meeting again, later, I could have been married, or he might not have been divorced, or something very small could have happened. The day we had coffee together one of us might have been nursing a cold, or depressed and the chance would have gone. Instead we had been lucky.

All through the fogs and the drizzle, until the air became firmer and the marigolds abandoned at the close mouth were feathered every morning with white, all through it, we learned about us. I remembered how new Michael could be. I would catch him, sometimes, smiling in a different light, or say goodbye to him and see him walk away and I would know there were things about him I hadn't begun to find out about yet. That pleased me.

Most of his past I knew, but I couldn't share. Some of the women I might have recognised in the street; certainly, if we'd had the chance to speak. I would have known the perfume, the way they liked to dress and, if they told me stories, I would have heard most of them before. There might be a new one, about this man with brown eyes and long hands who liked to keep chocolate in the fridge. At the end they would call him a bastard and look beyond my shoulder with a tired, short smile.

That was how I imagined it would be. I never had the

chance to try. I never met his wife. His ex-wife. Although I wanted to. I wanted to see if she was like him in ways that I was; to see what they had left of each other, and perhaps what would happen to us. Just to set my mind at rest. I told him it might be alright. He said I was perverse, so there you go.

My past was easy. Very short. School: my school friends still in touch enough to have a drink at Christmas, or other times a coffee, if we met. Summer holidays and birthdays and fat-kneed boys in kilts at dances and, almost in spite of everything, no sex. Michael was surprised at that. Sometimes pleased and sometimes guilty, but always surprised at that. The university bit he knew, because he was there and because, like a few of the others, he took an interest in the people he taught. It hadn't been so long, he would tell us, since he was one of us. I had five years to fill him in on: unemployed, then selling insurance, melting down new candles for the MSC and then getting the job. It took me ten minutes to tell him. The picture of me as a baby on the lopsided rug, the yellow-haired, dead father and the mother, he knew all of that.

We announced ourselves to mother, later. Like this.

It happened in the daft days. The New Year was over and the holiday nearly done, a yellow oil of lamplight over the rainy streets. We should have arrived in the summer with light clothes and smiles. Instead our faces were numb and raw, our fingers blind with the cold. We needed to have her tea, to be comfortable by her fire, on the sofa and Father's chair. By the time we had our wits about us, mother was ready.

'Go and fill the pot will you, darling.'

And away I went. I got back and she was interviewing Michael.

It wasn't that we hadn't expected it. It was a natural thing for her to do, but I wish that I could have said something when it happened. Something right. Instead I stood in the doorway, hardly listening, and thought of a book I'd found in Michael's flat. It was a hardback – Persian Art – I don't remember. And when I picked it out of the armchair to put it away I noticed a name and address and a date on the blank leaf at the front. It told me he had lived in a different city, in a house I didn't know and he had bought himself a book, priced in shillings when I was three years old. The nearest I can get to how I felt was how sad it was that he would die before me. How lonely I would be. I don't think, in her interview, mother ever mentioned that.

By the way, we hurt her. Not because of what we did, but because I hadn't told her. She hadn't known for all that time. I still saw her quite often with Michael and alone, but always she would speak to me as if I was a guest. She didn't trust herself to me; neither thought nor dream, and every time I saw her, she made me ashamed.

It was almost as if she had died and, perhaps because I had lost her or perhaps because of Mike, or both, I found that I wanted a child. I wanted to make it and have it, for it to be alive with the two of us.

My mother's pregnancy had ended very happily, laughing in fact. Mother had been watching a new Woody Allen film, I suppose I could find out which one, and suddenly, in a silence, she laughed. She laughed and found she couldn't stop laughing. Her laughing made her laugh. The worry in the face of my father, the little crowd of usherettes, the rush of figures who took her from the back of the cinema to the ambulance; they all made her laugh.

She gave birth within the hour, one month early, still weeping and giggling, amazed, and thinking of that first, secret thing that started her laugh.

I was not born even smiling, only a little underweight.

I wanted a child. I wanted it born laughing, they wouldn't be allowed to make it cry. I would tell them and Mike would make sure. I would have asked him to. It would have been good.

Before the end, before I start on that, there are too many things that were good that I remember. Sitting here, the rungs of the bench are against my spine and a crowd of sparrows is rocking a holly tree, but, behind them, it is quiet. Very quiet. There is space.

I always seem to think of Michael in the kitchen. He is at his clearest then, perhaps because we were busy together there, visiting each other, interrupting, letting things boil. I can smell the wet earth from the potatoes, our red, clay soil. He takes oranges and orange scent from a brown paper bag.

'Fifty pence for five. That's not bad. They're big.'

'You're mean, you know that? I've noticed.'

'They're big oranges, look. I'm not mean.'

'You're stingy.'

'Nice, cheap oranges. I am not stingy.'

'You're a stingy, grouchy, old man.'

He was wearing the big coat, the blue one. It smelt of evening weather and the car. I slipped my arms inside it and around his waist. That was something I did a lot.

'You're just after my oranges.'

'That's right.'

Michael stood very still for a while. He said,

'You do make me happy sometimes. You don't know.'

The dinner was good, with oranges after.

If I'd come to the park last week the afternoon would have been longer, but evenings come in fast now. You can see the change from day to day. By the time I get home the lights will be in the windows and Michael will be back, the fires on. He doesn't like the house to be cold.

I will tell him then. I think I will tell him.

I went there because it's a public service. In the student days we came for the tea and biscuits, but it felt good afterwards, just the same. You knew you could have saved a life. You hadn't run into a burning building or pulled a child out of the sea, but part of you had been taken and it would help someone. I liked it when they laid you on your bed with so many other people, all on their beds, all together with something slightly nervous and peaceful in the air.

They would talk to you and find a vein, do it all so gently, and I would ask for the bag to hold as it filled. The nurse would rest it on my stomach and I would feel the weight in it growing and the strange warmth. It was a lovely colour, too. A rich, rich red. I told my mother about it and she laughed.

I gave them my blood a couple of times after that, then my periods made me anaemic and then I forgot. I don't know what made me go back to start again.

Nothing much had changed, only the form at the beginning which was different and longer and I lay on a bed in a bus near the shopping centre, not in a thin, wooden hall.

Afterwards they send you a certificate. It comes in the post and you get a little book to save them in, like co-op stamps. This time they sent me a letter instead. It was a kind, frightening letter which said I should come and see someone; there might be something wrong with my blood.

I am full of blood. My heart is there for moving blood. The pink under my fingernails is blood. I can't take it away.

And now I am not what I thought I was. I am waiting to happen. I have a clock now, they told me that. A drunk who no longer drinks is sober, but he has a clock because every new day might be the day that he slips. His past becomes his achievement, not his future. I have a clock like that. I look at my life backwards and all of it's winding down. I think that is how it will stay. I think that's it.

Should I say it to Michael like that? Should I tell him that thing I remember about the American tribe. Those Indians.

They thought that we went through life on a river, all facing the stern of the boat and we only ever looked ahead in dreams. That's what I'll have to do now.

I think he told me about that. It sounds like him. It would give us some kind of start for the conversation.

Night Geometry and the Garscadden Trains

O ne question.
Why do so many trains stop at Garscadden? I
don't mean stop. I mean finish. I mean terminate. Why do so
many trains terminate at Garscadden?

Every morning I stand at my station, which isn't
Garscadden, and I see them: one, two, three, even four in a
row, all of them terminating at Garscadden. They stop and
no one gets off, no one gets on; their carriages are empty,
and then they pull away again. They leave. To go to
Garscadden. To terminate there.

I have never understood this. In the years I have waited
on the westbound side of my station, the number of trains to
Garscadden has gradually increased; this increase being
commensurate with my lack of understanding. The trees
across the track put out leaves and drop leaves; the seasons
and the trains to Garscadden pass and I do not understand.

It's stupid.

So many things are stupid, though. Like the fact that the
death of my mother's dog seemed to upset me more than the
death of my mother. And I loved my mother more than I
loved her dog. The stupidity of someone being killed by the

train that might normally take them home, things like that. There seems to be so much lack of foresight, so much carelessness in the world. And people can die of carelessness. They lack perspective.

I do, too. I know it. I am the most important thing in my life. I am central to whatever I do and those whom I love and care for are more vital to my existence than statesmen, or snooker players, or Oscar nominees, but the television news and the headlines were the same as they always are when my mother died and theirs were the names and faces that I saw. Nations didn't hold their breath and the only lines in the paper for her were the ones I had inserted.

Inserted. Horrible word. Like putting her in a paper grave.

To return to the Garscadden trains, they are not important in themselves; they are only important in the ways they have affected me. Lack of perspective again, you see? Naturally, they make me late for work, but there's altogether more to them than that. It was a Garscadden train that almost killed my husband.

Of course you don't know my husband, Duncan, and I always find him difficult to describe. I carry his picture with me sometimes; more to jog my memory than through any kind of sentiment. I do love him. I do love him, even now. I love him in such a way that it seems, before I met him, I was waiting to love him. But I remember what I remember and that isn't his face.

Esau was an hairy man. I remember my mother saying that. It always sounded more important than just saying he was born with lots of hair. I only mention Esau now, because Duncan wasn't hairy at all.

He had almost no eyebrows, downy underarm hair and a disturbingly naked chest. We used to go walking together as newly weds, mainly on moorland and low hills where he'd been as a scout. The summers were usually brief, unsettled, the way you'd expect, but the heat across the moors could be remarkable. It seems to be a quality of moors. The earth is warm and sweaty under the wiry grass, the heather bones are brilliant white and the sun swings, blinding, overhead. You walk in a cloud of wavering air and tiny, black insects.

On such days – hot days – Duncan would never wear a T-shirt. Not anything approaching it. He would put on a shirt, normally pale blue or white, roll the sleeves up high on his arms and wear the whole thing loose and open like a jacket, revealing a thin, vulnerable chest. Sensible boots, socks, faded khaki shorts and the shirt flapping; he would look like those embarrassing forties photographs of working class men at the beach or in desert armies. He had a poverty stricken chest, pale with little boy's skin.

There was hair on his head, undoubtedly, honey brown and cut short enough to subdue the natural curl, but his face was naked. I remember him washing and brushing his teeth, but I don't believe he ever shaved. There was no need.

Duncan, you might also notice, is in the past tense – not because he's dead, because he's over. I call him my husband because I've never had another one and everything I tell you will only show you how he was. Today I am a different person and he will be, too. Whatever I describe will be part of our past. I used to want to own his past. I used to want to look after him retrospectively. This was during the time when our affair had turned into marriage but still had something to do with love. In fact, there was a lot of love about. I mean that.

My clearest memory of him comes from about that time. I don't see it, because I never looked at it. I only remember a feeling, safe and complete, of lying with him, eyes closed, and whispering that I wanted to own his past; that I wanted to own him, too.

It was strange. However we flopped together, however haphazardly we decided to come to rest, the fit would always be the same.

His right arm, cradling my neck.

My head on his shoulder.

My right arm across his chest.

My left arm, tucked away between us with my hand resting quietly on his thigh. Not intending to cause disturbance, merely resting, proprietary.

In these pauses, we would doze together before sleeping and dreaming apart and we would whisper. We always whispered, very low and very soft, as if we were afraid of disturbing each other.

'I love you.'

'Uh hu.'

'I do love you.'

'I know that. I feel that. I love you, too.'

'I want to look after you.'

'You can't.'

'Why not.'

'Because I'm looking after you.'

'That's alright, then.'

'I love you.'

'Uh hu.'

'I do love you.'

And, finally, we would be quiet and sleepy and begin to breathe in unison. I've noticed since, if you're very close to anything for long enough, you'll start to breathe in unison. Even my mother's dog, when he slept with his head on my lap, would eventually breathe in time with me. There was more to it than that with Duncan, of course.

I sometimes imagined our hearts beat together, too. It's silly, I know, but we felt close then. Closer than touch.

This positioning, our little bit of night geometry, this came to be important in a way I didn't like because it changed. I didn't like it then, as much as I now don't like to remember the two of us together and almost asleep, because, by fair means or foul, you can't replace that. Intensity is easy, it's the simple nearness that you'll miss.

The change happened one evening on a Sunday. We had cocoa in bed. I made it in our little milk pan and I whisked it with our little whisk, to make it creamy, and we drank it sitting up against the pillows and ate all butter biscuits, making sure we didn't drop any crumbs. There is nothing worse than a bed full of crumbs. And we put away the cocoa mugs and we turned out the lights and that was fine. Very nice.

But when we slowed to a stop, when we terminated, the geometry had changed. I didn't really think about it because it was so nicely changed.

My right arm around his neck.

His head against my shoulder.

His one arm tucked between us very neat, and the other, just resting, doing nothing much, just being there.

It all felt very pleasant. The good weight of him, snuggled down there, the smell of his hair when I kissed the top of his head. I did that. I told him I could never do enough, or be enough, or give enough back and I kissed the top of his head. I told him I belonged to him. I think he was asleep.

I told him anyway and he was my wee man, then, and I couldn't sleep for wanting to look after him.

The following morning, I waited on the westbound platform and the smell of him was still on me, even having washed. All that day when I moved in my clothes, combed my hair, his smell would come round me as if he'd just walked through the room.

It was good, that. Not unheard of in itself, hardly uncommon, in fact. It wasn't unknown for me to leave my bed and dress without washing in order to keep what I could of the night before, but you'll understand that, this time, I was remembering something special. I thought, unique.

Now I realise that you can never be sure that anything is unique. You can never be sure you know enough to judge. I mean, when Pizzaro conquered the Incas, they thought he was a god – his men, too – when really Spain was full of Spaniards just like him. Eventually you see you were mistaken, but look what you've had to lose in order to learn.

I thought that the way I met Duncan was unique.

Wrong.

Not in the place: a bar. Not in the time: round about eight. Not in the circumstances: two friends of friends, talking at a wee, metal table when the rest of the conversation dipped. It was a bit of a boring evening to tell the truth.

We all left on the bell for last orders and there was the usual confusion about coats – who was sitting on whose jacket, who'd lost gloves. Duncan and I were a little delayed, quite possibly not by chance.

'I'm going to call you tomorrow. Ten o'clock. What's your number?'

'What?'

'What number could I get you on, tomorrow at ten o'clock?'

'In the morning?'

'Yes, in the morning.'

'Well, I would be at work, then.'

'I know that, what's the number?'

I gave him the office number and he went away. I don't even think he said goodbye.

At a quarter to eleven, the following day, he called McSwiggin and Jones and was put through to me. I had some idea that he might be in need of advice. McSwiggin and Jones accepted payment from various concerns with money to call in the debts of various individuals without it. Debt, as Mr McSwiggin often said, could be very democratic – Mrs Gallacher with two small boys, no husband and her loan from the Social Fund turned down was in debt. And so was Peru. Perhaps, I thought, Duncan was in debt.

'What do you mean, in debt?'

'I mean, who do you owe money? I can't help you if it's on our books. I mean I can, but not really, you know.'

'No, I don't know. I owe my brother a fiver, since you ask.'

'Mm hm.'

'And that's it. I don't have any debts, just a bit of an overdraft which doesn't count. I want to see you tonight. I could bring my bank statement with me if you'd like.'

'Look, I'm sorry, but you're wasting my time, aren't you?'

'I'm sorry if you feel that way. I thought we got on well together.'

'Ring me at home tomorrow evening. This is ridiculous and I'm at work.'

He called at the end of the week and we went out for a coffee on the Sunday afternoon. Before I had time to ask he told me that he and Claire, his partner from the pub, were only friends. They'd been at school together which is why they'd seemed so close the other evening.

When Duncan and I were married, quite a while later, Claire was at the little party afterwards. She smiled quietly when she saw me, danced with Duncan once and then left. I had to ask who she was because she looked so familiar, but I couldn't remember her name.

So, Duncan and I were married and we were unique. Although men and women often marry as an expression of various feelings and beliefs and although they often go to bed together before, during and after marriage, the thing with Duncan and me was unrepeatable, remarkable and entirely unique. So I thought.

No one had ever married us before and we had never married each other. It was tactfully assumed that the going to bed had happened with other partners in other times, but they had never managed to reach the same conclusion. We were one flesh, one collection of jokes and habits and one smell. Even now, I know, the smell of my sweat and the taste of my mouth are not the same as they were before I met him. He will always be that much a part of me, whether I like it or not.

Even when two different friends in two different ladies toilets in two different bars told me that Claire and Duncan had been sleeping and staying awake together for months before I met him, I didn't mind. I didn't mind if they had continued to see each other after we met. I was flattered he had taken the trouble to lie. It didn't matter because he had left her for me and we had made each other unique.

Finally, of course, I realised the most original things about us were our fingerprints. Nothing of what we did was ever new. I repeated the roles that Duncan chose to give me in his head – wicked wife, wounded wife, the one he would always come back to, the one he had to leave and I never even noticed. I always felt like me. For years, I never knew that when he rested with his head on my shoulder, all wee and snuggled up, it was helping him to ease his guilt. Once or twice a year, it was his body's way of saying he'd been naughty, but he was going to be a good boy from now on.

And I was a good wife. I even answered the telephone with a suitably unexpected voice, to give his latest girlfriend her little shiver before she hung up. Like a good wife should.

All the time I thought I was just being married when, really, Duncan was turning me into Claire and the ones before and after Claire.

I lived with the only person I've met who can snore when he's wide awake, who soaked his feet until they looked like a dead man's, then rubbed them to make them peel. I've washed hundreds of towels, scaly with peelings from his feet. I've cooked him nice puddings, nursed him through the 'flu, stopped him trimming his fringe with the kitchen scissors and have generally been a good wife. Never knowing how Duncan saw me inside his head. It seems I was either a victim, an obstacle or a safety net. I wasn't me. He took away me.

But it wasn't his fault, not really. It was the E numbers in his yoghurt, or his role models when he was young. It was a compulsion. Duncan, the wee pet lamb, would chase after anything silly enough to show him a half inch of leg. From joggers to lady bicyclists to the sad looking Scottish Nationalist who sold papers round the pubs in his kilt. Duncan couldn't help it. It wasn't his fault.

I sound like an idiot, not seeing how things were for so long. I felt like an idiot, too. Nothing makes you feel more stupid than finding out you were wrong when you thought you were loved. The first morning after I discovered, it wasn't good to wake up. Over by the wall in the bedroom there was a wardrobe with a mirror in the door. I swung my legs out of bed and just sat. There I was; reflected; unrecognisable. I looked for a long while until I could tell it was me: pale and slack, round shouldered and dank-haired, varicose veins, gently mapping their way. You would have to really love me to like that and Duncan, of course, no longer loved me at all. I could have felt sorry for him, if I hadn't felt so sorry for myself.

I considered the night before and letting his head rest on my shoulder, knowing what I finally knew. It was as if I wasn't touching him, only pressing against his skin through a coating of other women. I'd felt his breath on my collar bone and found it difficult not to retch.

It had taken about a month to fit all the pieces together in my head. Nothing silly like lipstick on collars, or peroxide blonde hairs along his lapels: it was all quite subtle stuff. He would suddenly become more crumpled, as if he had started sleeping in his shirts, while his trousers developed concertina creases and needed washing much more regularly. The angle of the passenger seat in the car would often change and, opening the door in the morning, there would be that musty smell. And yet, for all the must and wrinkles, the fluff all over his jackets, as if they'd been thrown on the floor, Duncan would be taking pains with his appearance. When he walked out of the flat he'd never looked better and when he returned he'd never looked worse. Life seemed to be treating him very roughly, which perhaps explained his sudden interest in personal hygiene, the increasingly frequent washing and the purchase of bright, new Saint Michael's underwear. It's all very obvious now, but it wasn't then. Even though it had been repeating itself for years.

Duncan's infidelity didn't have all the implications it might have today. I didn't take a blood test, although I've watched for signs of anything since. Still, you can imagine the situation in the first few weeks with both of us constantly washing away the feel of his current mistress. We went through a lot of soap.

I suppose that I should have left him, or at least made it

clear that I'd found him out. I should have made sure that we both knew that I knew what he knew. Or whatever it was you were meant to make sure of. I didn't know. To tell the truth, it didn't really seem important. It was to do with him and things to do with him didn't seem important any more. I couldn't see why he should know what was going on inside my head when, through all the episodes of crumpled shirts and then uncrumpled shirts and even the time when he tried for a moustache, I had never had any idea of what Duncan was thinking.

I stayed and, for a long time, things were very calm. We finished with all of our washing, started to sleep at night and I managed to get the dryer to chew up six pairs of rainbow coloured knickers. Duncan went back to being just a little scruffy and always coming home for tea.

It wasn't going to last, I knew. It would maybe be a matter of months before the whole performance started up again and I wasn't sure how I would react to that. In the meantime I sorted out my past. I still worked at McSwiggin and Jones, but only for three days out of seven and instead of spending the rest of my week on housework or other, silly things I started to sit on the bed a lot and stare at that mirror door. I bought some books on meditation and, at night, when I felt Duncan sleeping, I used to breathe the way they told me to – independently. It wasn't easy, crumpling up a marriage and throwing it away, looking for achievements I'd made that weren't to do with being a wife, but I don't think I did too badly. For a while I was a bit depressed, but only a bit.

My future, and this surprised me, was much harder to redefine. All the hopes you collect: another good holiday abroad, a proper fitted kitchen, children, a child. Your future creates an atmosphere around you and mine was surprisingly beautiful. Duncan and I, retired, would grow closer and closer, more and more serene, there would be grandchildren, picnics, gardening and fine, white hair. There would be trust and understanding, dignity in sickness and not dying alone. We would leave good things behind us when we were gone. I can't imagine where it all came from, I only know that it was hard to give away.

Then, one Monday morning, there was an incident involving my husband and a Garscadden train.

I went down, as usual, to stand on the westbound platform, this time in a hard, grey wind, the black twigs and branches over the line, oily and dismal with the damp. I waited in the little, orange shelter, read the walls and watched the Garscadden trains. There were three, and a Not In Service and, for the first time in my life, I gave up the wait. I turned around, walked away from the shelter and went home. I wished it would rain. I wanted to feel rain on my face.

The hall still smelt of the toast for breakfast. I took off my coat and went into the bedroom, needing to look in the mirror again, and there they were, in bed with the fire on, nice and cosy: Duncan and a very young lady I had never met before. They seemed to be taking the morning off.

Duncan ducked his head beneath the bedclothes, as if I wouldn't know it was him, and she stared at the shape he made in the covers and then she stared at me.

I don't believe I said a single word. There wasn't a word I could say. I don't remember going to the kitchen, but I do remember being there, because I reached into one of the drawers beside the sink and I took out a knife. To be precise, my mother's old carving knife. I was going to run back to the bedroom and do what you would do with a carving knife, maybe to one of them, maybe to both, or perhaps just cut off his prick. That thought occurred.

That thought and several others and you shouldn't pause for thought on these occasions. I did and that was it. In the end I tried to stab the knife into the worksurface, so that he would see it there, sticking up, and know that he'd had a near miss. The point slid across the formica and my hand went down on the blade, so that all of the fingers began to bleed. When Duncan came in, there was blood everywhere and my hand was under the tap and I'm sure he believed I'd tried to kill myself. The idea seemed to disturb him, so I left it at that.

He drove me to and from the hospital and stayed that night in the flat, but, when he was sure I felt stable again, he went away and we began the slow division of our memories and ornaments. It was all done amicably, with restraint, but we haven't kept in touch.

And that, I suppose, is the story of how my husband was almost killed by one Garscadden train too many. It is also the story of how I learned that half of some things is less than nothing at all and that, contrary to popular belief, people, many people, almost all the people, live their lives in the best way they can with generally good intentions and still leave absolutely nothing behind.

There is only one thing I want more than proof that I existed and that's some proof, while I'm here, that I exist. Not being an Olympic skier, or a chat show host, I won't get my wish. There are too many people alive today for us to notice every single one.

But the silent majority and I do have one memorial, at least. The Disaster. We have small lives, easily lost in foreign droughts, or famines; the occasional incendiary incident, or a wall of pale faces, crushed against grillwork, one Saturday afternoon in Spring. This is not enough.

Bix

He knew he was about to think of Maggie. She was in the air and on the way like thunder. This time it was the sound of her kiss. A sound of eating, of biting ripe fruit, of drinking and licking him up as if he was something nourishing and hot. It was always unmistakable and so loud. You would suppose that, in the quiet of the night, a kiss might well be noticed, especially close by the ear, but their nights had never been quiet. The railway battered past their window on a cutting above the back court with trains running into the small hours and then dragging by for repairs. There were cars and cat fights and anxious dogs, the drunk man down the stair and air in the pipes and above it all, their breathing as they roamed about the bed. Still Maggie's kisses would echo and shout, driving all the rest of it away.

The time would arrive when they lay without sleeping, side against side, and he would touch her to feel the last of her sweat. Between the curve of her stomach and the bone of her hip he would circle with his fingertips, find the place, then brush and twirl across it: the other side, too. That gave her little shivers which she liked. Sometimes these would lower her into sleep and sometimes they would make her start again. You never knew which until it happened.

The rain was harder now, twisting down in the wind and lifting back off the pavements in a haze. His hair had been needing washed, but now it would just look wet. Better to have an umbrella, though, or a hat. He would walk over west a little and find a bar. He was going to have a drink.

His drinking hadn't made Maggie leave him. He was sober when she went away. They didn't know each other when he started and it didn't seem she'd noticed when he stopped. For a time, when he was newly dry, he made a point of taking Maggie to the pictures. He made sure to arrive in time to watch the adverts, to sit beside his wife as the screen was filled with ice and lemon and slender girls in bikinis, plunging through rum. All they ever seemed to advertise was salted nuts and booze and he sat and stared them out, unblinking. He wanted her to see that he was strong. Then, one evening, after something funny, not the kind of film that she enjoyed, Maggie turned to him as they left and reached the street.

'Well, I'm away to Preston's for a while. I haven't seen that crowd for ages, with you and your moods. Don't worry, I'll not be late. Not all of us can't handle it, you know.'

That was the end of the pictures. Him and his moods.

But she had loved him, she had loved him very well. She wanted to be pretty for him; she told him that, time and again. He could alter the length of her dresses, the shade of   29 her lips, with a couple of words. Such power. She had cut her hair as he suggested and kept her legs and underarms shaved smooth, even asked if he would like her shaved elsewhere. She would have done it, too. Probably waited to surprise him, calling him in to watch her lather up. Enough of that.

It was only very slowly that she changed, the process beginning with her mouth. One by one, all her vowel sounds seemed to stretch. She managed to make the word gas rhyme with arse. She was very careful not to say youse, but only you. Sometimes, she sounded so strangled and uncomfortable, that he had to laugh. That made her angry and so he told her she was fooling no one and that made her angrier still.

He thought for a while she had a lover and was taking these pains for him, as her dresses and perfumes were gradually transformed. Then he realised. Every time she left the house Maggie was outshining him. Contrary to popular belief, he had been the first to show his age: just a touch of weight that he lost again, the hair not thin, but certainly turning grey and, of course, he'd still been drinking then, so he was getting slow. On the other hand, she still looked good; they both knew it. Standing next to him, she looked even better. She had seen it all happening and made up her mind. She encouraged the little smiles, the admiring comments, but now she added to them, now she could have her public's sympathy. Poor woman; intelligent, attractive and stuck with a sagging drunk.

That wasn't fair. She'd known she was getting on a wee bit and splashed out, that was all. It was his fault if he hadn't measured up. Blaming your failures on other people was a thing his friends had told him not to do. These were the friends that had kept him on the wagon by getting him to understand himself. They had also told him not to look for reasons because knowing why you did a thing wasn't the way to stop; it was only a way of putting decisions off. Still, he'd thought enough about it by then to know that whatever the reason was, it wasn't his wife. He owed his friends a lot, perhaps his life. It was a shame he hadn't seen them for a while.

He marched through the fading shower and wished for one of those blue, unsteady days. They had walked out together often, Maggie and himself, enjoying such days. It had been Summer – it was now – but it was a brighter Summer then. On Sundays they would head along the broad road out of town with a whipping, directionless wind taking the heat out of the sun. It would push at their coats and twirl their hair and rush the clouds above them, so the light fell like someone playing with a switch.

Days like that you could feel the river. You knew it was there all the time, behind the houses, but then you could feel it, you could smell it turning into sea. Everything was moving West; you, the clouds and Maggie and the river. You could feel the river, how alive it might be, slipping in between the grey spaces where the dead yards used to be, the new, red brick apartments and the empty docks.

The only place near them that you could see the river was where they'd cleared an old yard away and left them with open ground and the stubble of walls. There the river didn't look much, just a wee, grey rectangle with sometimes flecks of sun to prove it was moving.

The woman beside him, for all those Sundays, was Maggie. He must have been awful to be with for her to grow so changed. At the time, he hadn't thought so, but that must have been the way of it.

He chose this bar because he was tired and his eyes had started to ache. When he pressed his fingers against them, only lightly against the lids, it hurt so much that it scared him and he stopped. The music here was American; big band stuff, Swing and Glen Miller, too late for his tastes. Not like his 78s: his wee collection with all his raw and bawdy, melancholy friends. He wished they would play Ella, Louis, Velma Middleton, but most of all, Frankie Trumbauer, or just anyone playing with Bix. Sweet Bix Beiderbecke. He sat down and stared at the table until he was sure he wouldn't cry.

The waitress was dressed like all the others. Green and white candy striped blouse, little green waistcoat, white apron, black trousers and a green bow tie. It made her look fat. She didn't smile, perhaps because he didn't. He picked a hot chocolate from the menu and looked across at the bar as she moved away. It was very clean, with mahogany stained wood and brass and mirrors, no ash trays, or beer mats and here he was, sitting in an armchair with his elbows on a marble table top and behind him, a white plaster statue of a woman, clutching a sheet in a way that covered neither of her tits. She looked uncomfortable and Greek. They had a nice wind-up gramophone, a Columbia, some pseudo Thirties junk and several clocks, but they also looked uncomfortable and they made the rest of the place seem too new. It was all like their music: digital Glenn Miller and schmaltz. They wouldn't know real style from a kick in the head. And he was angry for being expected to feel out of place. Next time round he'd have a half and a whisky and then they'd see. People like them had been safe since he'd got sober.

Maggie would have liked it here, in fact, she probably did. It wasn't too far from her office. She must have come in. She would arrive with the girls, the ones that she needed to please, four or five of them, all laughing, in broad shouldered jackets and tight, little matching skirts. If they went after work, then Maggie would take a wee drink. A double Grouse, straight, no ice. Then she would take another and then she would start.

Indeed? I wouldn't have thought so.

That was what she always said and the people who were with her; strangers, acquaintances, friends; they wouldn't know what to expect. They wouldn't know that, if Maggie hadn't thought it, then the thing could not be so. But she never argued, that was a thing she didn't do. Maggie gave you the facts as she saw them and if you didn't agree, she   33 would give you them again, only this time, more slowly, so that you would understand. She was right and you were daft and that was it.

People laughed, or were offended and, whichever way, they left. Maggie didn't know this hurt him; that he had once punched a man in a toilet because he had laughed at her and said it was a sin she was out without her mother. He would come back to their table with his round and he would feel ashamed. She made herself so ugly and stupid and loud. Back home he would be angry because she had made him ashamed of his own wife and left him to brood on the guilt of that. It hadn't hurt his pride, that wasn't affected, he'd been surprised when someone had suggested that. He only hated being made ashamed.

The hot chocolate came in a white china mug with the name of the place around it in green letters. He wondered what kind of people came here. Who would arrange to meet in a place like this, with a name he would be embarrassed to say out loud? The waitress took his money, there and then, as if she didn't trust him not to leave without paying.

He decided he would leave without drinking. They would clear away the mug, still full, and cold, with a skin across it from the milk and that would let them know how much he thought of them. He would go away. This wasn't the place.

The evening he made her go he wanted to kiss her. He wanted to put his lips on her lips and lick between her teeth with his tongue. To feel the way she was snug and hard against him, comfortable and living and new, and to be surprised in the way he was always surprised when she tasted so much like him, he wanted that. He would have lifted her skirt and pulled her tight in and told her she was beautiful, but he couldn't do that. Not one part of that, could he do.

'Maggie. Maggie? Listen. Could you? Please?'

They had been watching television, a documentary about turtles and their eggs. He had sat a few feet away from her, knowing she was there and he must tell her, while the thousands of soft, baby turtles emerged from their sandy nests and began to die. Those who had escaped the egg thieves were mainly eaten or shrivelled up, as they pattered their way to the sea where most of the remainder would be killed. It made him depressed. He chose to tell her then. More than anything, to stop himself thinking of turtles all night.

'Maggie?'

'What is it?'

'I was talking to you.'

'I know. Can't it wait ten minutes for the end? Anyway, you know where the kettle is.'

This was the woman he had married because he had wanted to. She had carried her joy and love for him like a baby. The nursing of it had made her a second Mary, beautiful and serene and making the flesh and blood children they couldn't have superfluous. Or so it seemed.

She had been his glory.

'I don't want a cup of tea. I want to talk.'

'Not now. It's nearly time for bed. Tomorrow evening. I'm tired now, alright? You always pick your moment, don't you?'

'I know that, I'm sorry.'

'Oh, for Christ's sake. I'll go and put the kettle on. Just don't you bloody shift yourself, will you.'

And so the news he had caught her, as she opened the sitting room door.

'Barbara that I work beside, you don't know her. For two years, we've been screwing. I'm sorry. You'll want a divorce.'

Maggie never spoke. She just stood there and he didn't try to look at her face, so he couldn't remember now how it had been. A handful of turtles finally swayed out to sea and he heard her breathing, as if she was winded, and then she left.

At one point, he heard her call a taxi and, when it blew its horn, she came down the stair with two cases. He was waiting.

'You'll be away to your mother's. I understand. Tell her that I'm sorry, because I am.'

She put down her cases and punched the side of his head, in what seemed one continuous movement. Then her knee came up sharp against his balls, none too squarely, but enough, and she was gone.

That night, or to be more exact, the following morning,

when the luminous blue of a clear dawn was rising into his house, he tried to phone her. He had sweated out the night in a haunted bed. The hollow weight of her absence beside him kept him awake more completely than her presence ever had. The smell of her had lain all around him and so he had changed the sheets, pulled off the pillow slips, found a fresh coverlet, but she was still there. As soon as he started to doze, she would brush against him and he would feel the small disturbance of her breath.

By the telephone in the hall it was cooler. His mouth was bitter and sticky and a sick, dragging tiredness made the room swing whenever he turned his head, but he would call her and she would answer, because she was his wife and would know it was him calling because of what time it was. Probably she couldn't sleep herself.

But he couldn't dial the number. Then, when he did dial, he imagined he'd got it wrong and cut himself off before he was half way through. He dialled again and the number was right and again he couldn't let the call connect. He stopped dialling. A pulse had started up in his stomach and his hands began to shake. He let himself slide down the wall, let it chill his back, and he sat on the floor with the telephone held in his hands. His first day without her was coming and was cold and he didn't know how he could call her and he didn't know what he could say. He found that he was crying and it hurt.

He got through later, he didn't know how much later, and the line was engaged. Every time, engaged. It made him 37 feel stupid and alone.

There was no more rain, the cloud was breaking up and it was colder. It would be a cold night. He cut between the flowers, across the square, and spat. The sound was good, definite, and he wanted to be rid of something, if only that. Also, Maggie had hated him to spit. Across the road, there was the station, all lit up.

Many married men love other women and have neat affairs. Many men lie to their wives with great success. Their secrets are slowly forgotten and their marriages remain intact. How many men tell their wives they have loved elsewhere when this is a hurtful lie and will make them leave? But he had done that. He had made all of her leave: her soft, hot feet, her perms and highlights, the taste of stale whisky, waiting in her gentrified mouth. One evening, back from Preston's, she had kissed him like that. He remembered her slack, wet lips and her little, fat tongue; stubby and tangy with scotch.

Lips that touch liquor shall never touch mine.

And he pushed her away. She had woken him that night with an elbow in his ribs which had left a bruise. Gradually, he became aware of her, lying on her back, rocking and jerking and letting out moans. He had turned to her and kissed her shoulder, caught her hands.

'What are you doing?'

'What do you think? It's a better time than I ever get with you. Go back to sleep and leave me alone.'

A little while later he heard her come, then felt her settle down to sleep. He thought he should shake her awake again and fuck her; she'd still be wet. Then it came, still and clear in his mind, that he would sleep now, too, and be rid of her entirely, later on. In the process, if he could hurt her, he would be pleased.

There was no one that he worked beside called Barbara. In his life he had slept with three other women, all of them before Maggie, and once he was engaged, he had, as they said in the songs, been constant and true. He was not, he thought, faithful by nature, but his love for Maggie, really, love, and then later his isolation from suitable female friends, had meant he remained constant and true. From the times when this would set her weeping in his arms, they moved to her snide, over confident days, when she told him, among other people, that his bottle was all away to Hell. And there were other things she said he no longer had: it was odd that she should knee him in them, when she'd always been so certain they were gone. Just making sure, no doubt.

He stepped into the station, smiling. The place was mostly deserted; one sleeping train, a few people walking with coffee in paper cups, or just waiting for others to come, or themselves to go. He knew there was a bar here. It took its name from a well-known Scottish river, now flanked by decaying industries and sites for exclusive housing developments. The river he was born by. He went in.

A middle aged woman in white stilettos picked her way to the toilets at the back of the room. Her heels were unevenly worn, so she tottered and sometimes slid. Lieutenant Columbo watched her from the television set above the fruit machine.

She was almost the only woman, apart from the one behind the bar, and he felt at home. It was right being here. It was like what he'd seen in a film once where the restaurant at an airport had tables for the passengers in transit sectioned off. They had left but they hadn't arrived yet, so they were nowhere and they were kept away from the others in case the nowhere spread. He remembered that.

This was a nowhere; a less expensive one. You could drink here until you couldn't drink any more and stand here until you couldn't stand any more and you needn't be sad or angry when nobody cared. There was nobody here to. Nobody to be guilty, or ashamed. No body. No where.

Shite. He should just order and make a start.

Then he was afraid. He shouldn't do this. He couldn't trust himself to do this, because he knew that he couldn't be trusted, that this had been shown. The brandy glass with the china cat peering over the lip had shown it. In the morning it had been smashed and in the fireplace; the china cat, a headless, tailless cat; as if it had been hit by a china car. He didn't find a replacement for that, although with many other things, he did. The bruise around Maggie's eye with the tiny cut had sorted itself. He could only cry when he woke and saw that, not remembering how it had happened, but knowing it must have been him. Sometimes he lost his grip on things a little, that was a fault.

But all of that had stopped. The breaking and the drinking had stopped and he had bought her new things. Then she set in with her dusting and methodically, maliciously, broke them all. He had replaced almost everything and bought her other presents besides and she had broken them all. In the end, he believed there was nothing left to break; hearts being soft, pulsing organs, only broken in songs. Then Maggie had come back and broken his songs.

There was no way of telling when. It could have been only a day after she left him, it could have been when she came back to fetch her things, it could have been any time when he was out, because she kept her key. Whenever and however, by degrees or all in one rush, Maggie had gone to his cupboard and done this thing, intentionally, to hurt him. She had taken out each of his 78s, felt the fat, black weight of them, seen the ripple in the fine grooved surface, like satin or watered silk, and she had broken every one. Not smashed, broken into large, irregular pieces all of which had been fitted together again and replaced in their brittle, paper sleeves.

Bix Beiderbecke was broken. All of him. Bix, the inspirational, the biting, unrepeatable, lyrical Bix. Bix, whose parents had sat at home, his letters to them unopened, thinking of piano lessons wasted. Bix who was fond of a wee refreshment, who liked his drink. Bix who died young and made things alright because drunks who died young were romantic; they'd paid for the damage they'd done. It wasn't as good if you managed to stay alive.

When he found what had happened he hadn't known what to do. He went through them all when he discovered. Columbia, HMV, Brunswick, Parlophone; sleeves advertising needles and gramophone repairs, he searched through them slowly, then fast, then very slowly, as he knew he was coming to the end. All gone. Maggie was a very thorough woman. He had truly hated her then. Things had not been right with him ever since.

Bix was gone.

The Seaside Photographer

I came to the library and I don't know why.

There's an old man behind me and he's breathing like a big cat in a cage. It's a loud, fierce breath that should come with running, with pulling back at the anger before you fight, with making love. This man is blue round his lips and gasping from sitting in a chair and reading the morning's paper.

I came to be in the library and I don't know why. The air is full of reading and now you can't read and I didn't think of that before I got here. I just came to the library, not knowing why.

This was a good day. The umbrella has stayed in my bag, telescoped and rolled up tight. Dawn started slowly. And I was up to see it rise; the milky blue dawn, clear and almost chill, that brought in a hot, sweet afternoon. It is now a very gentle evening and, if I could see them, the clouds would be blushing or burning, or sculling off with the sun, towards the west. Whichever would be the most appropriate.

When I don't have a book of my own, I read Ed McBain. Whatever they have with his name on I read until it's time

43

for me to leave and each of the unfinished pieces has collided and combined. There are severed heads in airline holdalls and burnt up bodies tied with wire. When I read them, I liked the characters and the way he talks about Spring, but afterwards, it's the pathology that clings. There'll be a reason for that, but I don't know it.

Twice I've ever seen you with a book. The first one you set on the windowsill as soon as I came into the sitting room, because you always preferred to talk. That was a Western with a desert coloured cover and its price in pence and shillings on the front. You gave me the second one later, when I couldn't get to sleep. It was an Alistair MacLean, I think, quite new. I didn't like it and I still couldn't sleep.

You keep watch in the night, you always have. I remember your coughs and the creaking, you slipping into the toilet to have a smoke and shadowing out to the back to look at the night. I knew. I heard you. You never slept. McBain might not have suited you, might not have been just right, but I wish I had given you something then, to save you from the dark.

For me it happened today, this good day. I woke, having dreamed a little, and washed and spent hours full of the small things to do with me. I worked. Also, I answered the telephone. It told me how different your day had been. This day and how many before it.

I wanted to call you and say things, or say nothing and hope that you would know.

I don't understand what I should do.

I have you in my head and it's all lies. Not memories, lies. You are walking through the snowy zoo with your black umbrella, striding with it furled, wanting to show me the bears, or the parrots. I am in the shadow of your overcoat, my hand in the pocket of your overcoat, down among the tickle of cellophane and peppermints and I am warm. It feels like Good King Wenceslas and I'm wishing for a blizzard to come, to let me step in your footprints and still be warm. Later, at the bus stop, I can wrap both my arms around one of yours and let it lift me up. I can swing.

But this leads me to other places now, to a path between woods, under sugar loaf cones of orange lamplight and warm rain where I walked with my fingers laced in other fingers and our hands in the pocket of his rain coat while he talked. It was the last night we could have before he went away. My third time ever and every time with him.

Each of these things makes the other one a lie. There is nothing to keep them apart, these lies, year, on year, on year, and each one becomes another. Except that I see his face as I can see it today and your face is fifteen years out of date. You are not in my dreams, as he is, but I love you both.

When I was young I thought you had everything you wanted. You'll remember once, I asked if you were rich. It wasn't out of greed, not even curiosity, I was sure in my heart that you were a millionaire. I just wanted the thrill of hearing you say it out loud. I would have kept it to myself. I didn't know that you would always give, whether you were   45 able to or not. I didn't know what you did when I wasn't there. To me, you could not have been anything but happy and certain and wanting to give, because you were made like that.

A while ago I watched another man turn to walk away on a summer street and if he had been a child of mine, straying too near to the kerb, not quite safe, I would have felt the same. Just for a moment I wanted to call him back. The way you always want to call them back, to say something, anything. To wish them well, although they won't understand it if you do. You would have watched me like that, without my understanding. You were only the same as everyone else. Not rich, not always happy, not always certain, not born to be safe. And you had no power.

I realised that sooner and younger than anything else and you know that I blamed you. I thought you had made a decision to be weak, that you could make that decision, and that it was your fault. When you said they should call off all the wars and work it out with the gloves on, up in the ring, it was you that I saw. Your hair in a glossy black crew cut, with the flag a discreet block of colour on the shine of your white vest, high boots and long shorts, the saviour of your nation. Of course, you hadn't fought for years; not since before I was born, but you still had the build and the faith in your muscle. I believed in your faith.

I stood next to you in your kitchen and leaned the way you were leaning, over the window, over the edge. I made it

so that our shoulders were touching and feeling the warmth

through your shirt made me shiver as we looked out the back. Through the window it was icy mist and your cigarette threaded out to join it and there was dead quiet out there, like the ghost of a dawn.

My mouth was still tasteless with sleep and my eyes kept yawning back and trying to close and you said to me,

I thought you were going to stay longer,

and kept on looking out. I couldn't think of any words.

So my father led me away, past the bed that we would have made later and that would have been still warm from where I'd slept. I knew that you weren't going to stop him, that's why I never asked. I never even cried.

You couldn't stop your daughter's husband, like you couldn't stop the wars.

I'm sorry. I don't think as sorry as you.

The things that made you, I'll never see. You told me all about London before the war, when you were the champion of the works; the Black Country apprentice, taking all comers on. There was the time when the man got caught in the overhead belts and went up and round and was dead before they got him down. You didn't talk much about it, but I remember. Everyone else had gone to bed and I was up late, listening, when you said about the white hot bar and the way it just touched the chest of this one man and went straight on through. You looked at his back and saw daylight before he fell.

After that you stopped yourself in case you gave me dreams. You didn't. I felt the same way that I did when you took me down to your work. A Sunday, no one else there and, I don't know how, but you let us in and the whole place was as if it belonged to you. Every one of those machines you understood, and you could set all that heaviness in motion at a touch. You could conjure up whirling and screaming that filled the shop and set strange new components slithering out, still hot. You pattered me along the corridors left between the machines and all of it was waiting for the switch to set up a roar, with the bitter smell of sweat and metal stirred up everywhere we stepped.

Just for the afternoon you were the master and the owner and the magician for me. We kept that our secret afterwards.

I don't know what made you how you are. I wasn't there on the day you decided there were changes you could no longer make and now you would stay with turn-ups, stay with flannel for underwear and after Heath, you would stop voting and each year would put you closer to your past.

Now there is a change for the worst. I don't understand how these things happen. Perhaps you took too many punches and they hurt inside your head, perhaps the little sparks of iron that caught you were finally too much, or perhaps it was always being patient, only letting the pressure show with the tap and tap and tap from your nervous foot in the dark of the room. All these cancers you collect through time; they are in you but not of you and yet part of what people think of, whenever they think of you.

They are as real as you. Each one of them could be a reason, it could be none of them, it could be all. Whatever the cause you are blind now. Suddenly.

I have no magic for you and there is nothing I have learned to make. If, in this world, I could, I would write you whole and well. I would write you smiling through windy sunshine and strolling with your wife, the thin boards of the promenade beneath you, reaching up to a seaside photographer. I would wish myself unborn and you as you were in a holiday picture. A picture I have lost.

As it is, you are more and better now than ever you were then, a more beautiful and perfect, breathing man. Nothing should dare touch you, not a thing. Only, the years and the years' hardness, they were out and waiting for you from the start.

All I can do is write you words you cannot read and feel them between us.

Genteel Potatoes

This is no more than a story about Grandmother, because it cannot be the truth. If you and I were there to see it now, it might be the truth, but as it is, this is a story. Time divides me from my mother and her mother and beyond them there are lines and lines of women who are nothing more than shadows in my bones. And as you read this I am somewhere else. So this is a story.

In this story Grandmother will be afflicted by both her future and her past and the detail of her surroundings will be sadly incomplete. She will be there, perhaps with arthritic hands and a young girl's face, in a dress of no particular colour or shape, the streets around her very quiet, unsure of their proper sound.

Grandmother's age in the story is unclear. She is no younger than ten and no older than thirteen and is one of her parent's very many children. So far only one of them has died. Grandmother has no idea of which ones will leave the country and be buried in Canada, which ones will marry, which one will kill himself. She doesn't know them all that well.

Foremost among her numerous brothers and sisters are

Edgar, Ivy and Sue.

Edgar, though only a boy, is bald-headed, stout and troubled very much with sciatica. He wears khaki overalls that smell of the turkeys he will keep.

Ivy is plump, cheerful, good at the waltz. She will have both of her hip joints replaced after an eighteen month wait, will make wonderful apple dumplings and be poor. She will be poorer than all of them, and almost all of them will be poor.

Sue, during the war, the Second War, that is, will find a severed head in the alley behind the house. The morning after the sugar works is bombed. What she will do with the head we do not know, but my mother will one day remember it when she sees another, severed head in a car crash in Dundee. No one she recognised.

Grandmother's mother who is one, whalebone stiff photograph today, will make my mother drink castor oil each time she goes to the dentist and once chased Grandmother all round the house with a riding crop for acknowledging the sex of the household cat, or for saying a pregnant lady was going to have a child. Possibly both. In these days suitable topics for conversation among young girls were rather restricted and the restrictions were rather vigorously applied.

And on this particular day of all those days, Grandmother – skinny, long-fingered, big-footed and possibly thirteen – would wake in the morning to the world of work. Her mother had told her that she would.

It had been decided that Grandmother's schooling had come to an end and now she would go into service and bring back a wage. She would cook and clean for a genteel lady and her genteel family and, as their genteel house was not so very far away, Grandmother could even go home and sleep in her own bed at night. This was a Good Position and Grandmother should be glad.

Grandmother was not glad. Grandmother had already whitewashed the kitchen ceiling while two pulleys of clean washing swung, inches away from her brush, just to prove it could be done. And she left the washing spotless, too. Nevertheless, she was once again pursued with the riding crop. And caught. But still she remained a wilful soul, naturally awkward with never the faintest idea of her station in life.

Only severe persuasion moved Grandmother from the front doorstep, along the street, around the corner and on the way to her first day's work. A great many tears were shed in the process and when, despite her best efforts, she did not get hopelessly lost, but arrived at her new employer's, safe and sound, she must have been a pitiable sight. All skin and bone and wet, pink, rabbit eyes.

The genteel lady of the house took her in and explained her duties very carefully. The genteel family had graduated from paying someone else to do their washing to employing a genuine, full time, domestic assistant. They were thereforemost particular whenever they laid down the law so that all those concerned could be sure they were born to it.

The genteel lady smiled a little, genteel smile for Grandmother, who stood very still; frail and amenable.

The work was not difficult, or easy, only familiar. Grandmother didn't dislike it – she had done it all before at home – but somehow her position filled her with a wearying kind of shame. There was no shame in cleaning, or cooking; no shame in service if you took to it. What seemed to trouble Grandmother was that she had one idea of service and the genteel lady seemed to have another. Grandmother was ashamed for being too hesitant to point out that difference.

The shame and the difference preyed on her mind but still, she scrubbed and polished and dusted and made everything shine with a suitably genteel shine. Then it was dinner time.

In the genteel kitchen were the huge, copper pans and the glossy, black range, all glowing with admiration for Grandmother's efforts in the hours before. Here, it was explained, Grandmother would cook dinner for the family and for herself. There were the genteel potatoes and there were the ones she could have. The lady of gentility would return in a while to see how the work progressed.

Of course the lady of the house was not fully in possession of the facts. No one ever is, but in this particular case, her ignorance would soon be her undoing.

And what does she not know?

Why, what we know.

That Grandmother now is fast approaching her eightieth

year and yet she has never once, in all of that time, cooked an edible meal. That Grandmother is, undeniably, a wilful soul, naturally awkward with never the faintest idea of her station in life.

That means that, if the dinner is cooked, the family may not be poisoned, but they will be severely distressed. This also means that the dinner will never be cooked, because Grandmother is about to inspect the potatoes and find them wanting.

The genteel potatoes in the larger pile are soft and a little green and marked by careless lifting. Grandmother's very own potatoes are also soft and green and marked and, besides this, sprouting. Two of them have started to rot. Grandmother knows about potatoes. Her family keeps a little small holding and grows them. She is appalled by all these potatoes and appalled, more than anything else, by the potatoes which were set aside for her.

In her left hand, she snatches up a few of the family's potatoes. In her right, she flourishes two set aside for her; the soft rot from one of them, oozing through her fingers. Duly armed, she goes in search of her employer.

Bursting into the parlour, potatoes aloft, Grandmother fixes the genteel lady with one, magnificent glare. The same glare will, one day, wither tedious Methodist preachers at two hundred yards.

'See these?'

She will say, letting the middle class potatoes fall from her hand.

'We wouldn't feed these to our pigs.'

The family did keep pigs.

'And these . . .'

The proletarian potatoes make an overly soft landing on the rug and Grandmother is leaving her silence behind her. She has decided that she will resign. Nothing the genteel lady will ever say, and she will say a good deal, can change the fact that Grandmother resigned. She leaves voluntarily, shoulders back and remembering to take her coat. As she walks home there is no more shame and no more difference and the matter had been laid to rest.

Grandmother's mother will see her arriving home, hours too early, and go to fetch the riding crop. Grandmother's explanation will only make things worse and she will go to bed hungry, turn her back on her sister in bed and cry.

This won't be all her punishment. Next week she will be apprenticed to an old french polisher. He will be cruel to her, because he is a cruel man and because he is a drunkard. Worse than this, Grandmother knows that she will be a drunkard, too. She will have to take the methylated spirits in her mouth and spit them out between her teeth to leave an even spray across the wood and, in the end, she'll get a taste for the meths, because all of them do. For months she will be very tired and very afraid.

But Grandmother will be saved. Someone will invent a mechanical, pressurised spray and she will begin to love her strange, man's job. She will learn to recognise every variety of wood, no matter how cleverly disguised. She will pluck 55 out different shades of brown, like an eskimo identifying snow. She will make her living from almost invisible differences and will make each finished surface smoother than a dream of a whisper of a breath on silk. And still complain it's rough and shoddy work.

The first time she marries, no one will tell her that her husband has cancer and will die. He will be dead beside her the morning after their wedding night. It will be like a bad joke come true and nothing will be reliable again. For a long time she can't let herself be alone in her own home. She will willingly sit in the street in the rain, just to keep near to people as they pass.

Then Grandfather will marry her and love her very much and things will begin to get better, although never entirely the same. They will have their hair and their suits cut identically. Grandmother sports an Eton Crop for years. Their first and only child will be a daughter and her first and only child will be me.

That is how much will happen before Grandmother and I will even meet and before I can begin this story.

A Note on A. L. Kennedy

A. L. Kennedy was born in Dundee and lives in Glasgow. Her first book, *Night Geometry and the Garscadden Trains*, won the John Llewellyn Rees Prize and the *Scotsman* Saltire Award. Her second book of short stories, *Now That You're Back*, won an SAC Book Award. Her novels are *Looking for the Possible Dance*, winner of the Somerset Maugham Award, and *So I Am Glad*, winner of the *Scotsman* Saltire Award. She was listed among the *Sunday Times/Granta* Best of Young British Novelists.

Other titles in this series